John H Rhodes

The Gettysburg Gun

John H Rhodes

The Gettysburg Gun

ISBN/EAN: 9783337172237

Printed in Europe, USA, Canada, Australia, Japan

Cover: Foto ©Andreas Hilbeck / pixelio.de

More available books at **www.hansebooks.com**

THE

GETTYSBURG GUN.

BY

JOHN H. RHODES,

[Late Sergeant, Battery B, First Regiment Rhode Island

Light Artillery.]

PROVIDENCE:

PUBLISHED BY THE SOCIETY.

1892.

Alfred G. Gardner.

Born in Swansea, Mass., December 25, 1821.
Killed at the mouth of the Gettysburg gun, July 3, 1863.

THE GETTYSBURG GUN.

THE brass field piece which stands on the granite pedestal at the south side of the State House parade has a history unequaled perhaps by any other gun that did service in the war for the Union. An honorable history it is, for it was the prize for which, in that terrible battle of Gettysburg, brave men on both sides contended in a deadly hand to hand encounter. The battery boys, backed by the brave Sixty-ninth Pennsylvania, finally won the prize, but a dearly bought one it was, for it was paid for by the sacrifice of the lives of many gallant men.

The Gettysburg gun was one of the park of six brass field light twelve-pounder Napoleons of Battery B First Regiment Rhode Island Light Artillery, which the battery received at Harrison Landing, Va., in exchange for the ten-pounder Parrots with which the inner man for the work that was in prospect before them.

At five A. M. orders were received to move to the front, and the battery was soon in motion on the Taneytown road to Gettysburg, where we arrived about ten A. M., and were assigned position in battery on the left of the Second Corps line with General Harrow's First Brigade of Second Division on Cemetery Ridge, our left being joined by the Third Corps.

General Sickles advanced the Third Corps to the front about two P. M., thus creating a gap, and leaving the Second Corps exposed on its extreme left with only Battery B to fill the interval.

While the Third Corps was engaged at the Devil's Den and Peach Orchard in the struggle of the rebels for possession of Little Round Top, Battery B was advanced to the right and front a few hundred rods, about four P. M., upon higher ground in front of the main line, at the edge of a small wooded ridge, at General Gibbon's (Second Division of the Second Corps) left front, known as the "Godori's field," and went into battery at once, and opened fire upon a rebel

battery that had obtained a good range upon General
Meade's headquarters.   After a well directed fire of
about twenty minutes, the rebel battery could stand
our fire no longer and withdrew.   At this time the
rebels showed themselves in force at our left front
moving towards the battery, which the boys thought
to be our men of the Third Corps falling back ; but
after we had received their fire and heard that well
known "rebel yell" as they charged for our battery,
we were in doubt no longer, but sprang to the posts
at the guns ready to receive them.   This force of
the enemy proved to be General Wright's brigade of
General Anderson's division, making for the gap
between the Second and Third Corps.   The enemy
were in solid front of two lines of battle.   And as
our artillery fire cut down their men they would
waver for a second, then close up and continue to
advance, their battle flags fluttering in the breeze,
and the sun reflecting its dazzling rays from the bar-
rels of their muskets.

The violent forcing back of General Humphrey's
division of the Third Corps, brought destruction
upon the force under Col. George H. Ward, consist-

ing of his own regiment the Fifteenth Massachusetts,
the Eighty-second New York, Lieutenant-Colonel
Huston, and Battery B, which had by General Gib-
bin's orders been thrown forward to the Godori
house on the Emmittsburg road, to partially cover
the gap caused by the abrupt advancing of the Third
Corps.

As the enemy (Wright's brigade), advanced a
desperate resistance was made by this little band,
which was far overlapped on their flank, and at last
compelled to retreat.

As the enemy were forcing General Humphrey's
left back towards the line they first occupied, and
the position where the battery was first placed on
coming up to the front, General Hancock came gal-
loping up the line towards his right (going north),
and saw a portion of the enemy, (Wilcox's brigade)
coming out into the opening, from the cover of a
clump of bushes. He looked right and left for troops.
Turning round he saw a regiment coming up from the
rear. Dashing up to the colonel, and pointing to the
enemy's column he exclaimed : "Do you see those
colors ? Take them." And the gallant First Minne-

sota (Colonel Colville), sprang forward, and precipitated themselves upon the advancing foe, and three-fourths of the regiment were destroyed in the impetuous onset.   Thus was the gap partially closed, but on came the advancing foe.   Battery B began firing four second spherical case shell, that is, shell filled with small lead or iron bullets and powder enough to burst them.   (Ours contained about seventy in number.)   Battery B being in an exposed position, it received the concentrated fire of the enemy, who were advancing so rapidly that the fuses were cut at three, two, and one second, and then canister, and at last double charges were used to a gun.   Then came the order, "Limber to the rear;" and shouts from the infantry "Get out, you will all be killed." From the battery boys, it was, "Don't give up the guns."

During this time the foe were advancing and firing by volleys.   Having failed in the attempt to secure the gap, their objective point now seemed to be the capture of the battery, but the battery was well supported by the Sixty-ninth and One Hundred and Sixth Pennsylvania boys, and so succeeded in retiring with four pieces leaving two on the field, the horses having been killed. In retiring the battery came under a heavy enfilading fire from the wing of the flanking foe which had overlapped us, and before we could retire to the rear of the line of our support, for we had to go through a narrow gap in the stone wall which made breastworks for the infantry, and only one piece at a time,—we had many of our men and horses wounded.

As the sixth piece was approaching the gap it was forced to halt, as the gap was partially blocked by two pieces trying to go through at the same time. Before it was cleared, one of the horses on the sixth piece was killed and another wounded, so the drivers were forced to abandon the horses and gun, the enemy being right upon them, some lying down, some making for the gap, each side of which a vivid flame streamed, sending forth the messengers of death to the foe.

When the order was given "Limber to the rear," the fourth piece was loaded, the sergeant (Albert A. Straight) waited until it was fired before he repeated the order to limber up, and when he did, two of his horses were shot and fell so the order could not be executed; but he gave orders for the men to look out for themselves, the gun being left in position on the field, and this one is the so called Gettysburg gun, and not the sixth piece which was abandoned near the gap in the wall.*

The other pieces which reached the rear of our battle line got in battery at once, and opened fire again upon the advancing foe, but soon stopped firing to enable our infantry to charge. Then came a struggle for the possession of those guns.

The gallant Sixty-ninth Pennsylvania held their ground, and advanced with the brigade on the charge, drove the foe back and held the guns. When finally the rebs were driven back across the Emmittsburg road, the two pieces of Battery B were withdrawn from the field to the third position occupied by the

* In the diary of the sergeant of that piece under date of July 2, 1863, is written:

"We were ordered to limber to the rear when they (the rebs) had got very near to us, two of my horses got shot just as the order was given, and I could not get my piece off, and the boys had to look out for themselves as the Johnnies were all around us, and the bullets flew very lively, with some shot and shell, all my horses were killed, David B. King was hit and lived but a few minutes, and one man was taken prisoner. I got my piece again after the charge was over.

[Signed]   ALBERT A. STRAIGHT."

battery. After the charge the brigade fell back to
its old position on the ridge, at the wall.

The casualties of July 2d were three men killed,
one taken prisoner, and fifteen wounded. Thir-
teen horses were killed and a number wounded.
First Lieut. T. Fred. Brown was wounded as the
battery was withdrawing from the field, and the
command was assumed by First Lieut. William S.
Perrin.*

During this engagement our caissons, with full
complement of men and horses were parked in the
rear of the second line of infantry of the corps,
and remained undisturbed. It was therefore wholly
upon this account that the battery was enabled to
take part in the battle of the 3d of July with four
guns fully equipped.

Night closed the scene. White robed peace
flung her mantle, for a brief interval, o'er the victor
and vanquished, the dying and the dead. Hushed
was the fearful strife, and sleep closed the eyelids of
men weary and worn with battle. How many were

---

* [The horses as they lay on the field were not despoiled of their harnesses,
nor was the ammunition remaining in the limber chests taken by the rebels, as
has been stated, but all property was recovered intact.]

sleeping the last sleep of the living upon this earth, and what myriads of heavenly beings were wafting the thoughts of those sleeping soldiers back to the live ones, to the homes of their childhood days, and perhaps to the last sad parting. Morning came all too soon, for ere the golden orb of day had tinted the east with his splendor the call was to arms, to again look death calmly in the face and patiently wait the summons to battle. Stern duty lay before them, an enemy to conquer, and a government to honor and uphold.

The dawn of July 3d broke in splendor, but before the beauty of that magnificent landscape was revealed by the first rays of the sun, the clamor of human strife broke forth, and rose and swelled to fury along the rocky slopes of Culp's Hill on our right. The cause for this was, the Twelfth Corps returning from the left found their old position occupied by the enemy (Johnson's Division), and only waited for daylight to advance and drive the intruders out. The contest was sharp but the nature of the position did not permit of rapid and decisive work. Little by little the enemy was forced back until compelled to give up the ground and to abandon the position to the Twelfth Corps. In Battery B on the morning of July 3d, the four pieces were so posted that the centre pieces were a little in advance of the right and left pieces, so as to bear upon and command a given point. First Lieut. W. S. Perrin commanded battery and right section, Second Lieut. C. A. Brown commanded left section. The Seventy-second Pennsylvania Regiment, Colonel Baxter, lay to the left and rear of the battery in support. Lieutenant Cushing's battery A, Fourth United States, held position several rods to our right and a little in advance. Several rods to our left on the same line was Battery B, First New York in position.

During the morning a desultory fire of artillery was kept up, during which the rebels fire succeeded in exploding several ammunition chests of the gun limbers, and in return we retaliated and performed the same service for them, this being acknowledged by both parties with continued shouts and cheers.

As the forenoon wore on, there came a lull, a stillness even of death. A feeling of oppression weighed upon all hearts, the silence was ominous and

portentous of coming evil. It was the calm which
precedes the storm.

At one o'clock in the afternoon a cannon shot
from the enemy's line, from the Washington Artillery, was fired on our right followed by another at
an interval of a minute, breaking the silence brood-
ing over the scorched battlefield.

It was a signal well understood, and the smoke of
those guns had not dispersed before the whole rebel
line was ablaze, and over one hundred cannon sent
forth a concerted roar, that rivaled the angriest thunder. Our cannoneers jumped to their places at the
pieces, the drivers to their horses, waiting the order
to commence firing.

It was ten or fifteen minutes before we received
orders to fire. Then at the command, the shrieking
shot and shell were let loose upon their work of
destruction, proving to be one of the most terrible
artillery duels ever witnessed.

Then came Pickett's grand charge to break the
Union centre, sweep the Second Corps from their
path and then on to Washington. How Lee succeeded history tells.

It was during this fierce cannonade that one of the pieces of Battery B was struck by a rebel shell which exploded and killed two cannoneers. The men were in the act of loading it. No. 1, William Jones, had stepped to his place between the muzzle of the piece and wheel, right side, and had swabbed the gun and reversed sponge staff, which is also the rammer, and was waiting for the charge to be inserted by No. 2. Alfred G. Gardner, No. 2, had stepped to his place between the muzzle of the piece and wheel, left side, facing inward to the rear, taking the ammunition from No. 5 over the wheel. He turned slightly to the left, and was in the act of inserting the charge into the piece when a shell from one of the enemy's guns, struck the face of the muzzle, left side of the bore and exploded. William Jones was killed instantly by being struck on the left side of his head by a fragment of the shell, which cut the top completely off. He fell with his head toward the enemy, and the sponge staff was thrown forward beyond him two or three yards.

Alfred G. Gardner was struck in the left shoulder, almost tearing his arm from his body. He lived a

few minutes and died shouting, "Glory to God! I
am happy! Hallelujah!" his sergeant and friend
bending over him to receive his dying request.

The sergeant of the piece, Albert A. Straight,
and the remaining cannoneers tried to load the piece,
placing a charge in the muzzle of the gun. They
found it impossible to ram it home. Again and
again they tried to drive home the charge which
proved so obstinate, but their efforts were futile.
The depression on the muzzle was so great that the
charge could not be forced in, and the attempt was
abandoned, and as the piece cooled off the shot
became firmly fixed in the bore of the gun.

This piece is the so called Gettysburg gun of
Battery B, First Regiment Rhode Island Light
Artillery.*

*[Extract from a letter the sergeant of this piece wrote to his brother John,
dated July 7, 1863:

"We arrived near to Gettysburg, Penn., on the night of July 1st, and on
the 2d we had a fight. I had one man killed, David B. King, of my detachment,,
six horses killed and one wounded.

The rebels charged our battery and we had to retire a short distance to the
rear of our second line of infantry; our support in front gave way. But the rebels fared badly, for but few of them got back to tell the story, they were repulsed
with so terrible a loss. I also had one man missing; probably he was taken
prisoner, as the rebels were within a few paces of us when we left.
Lieutenant Brown commanding the battery was badly wounded, also Sergeant Chase and many others. But this was nothing to the next day's fight.

'By this letter it proves that the piece and carriage were struck three times, and that there was an explosion, for the sergeant says that his piece was struck three times by shot or shell before they exploded. Now they must have been shell which struck to have exploded. The writer distinctly remembers seeing the explosion at the piece when the two men were killed, but at the time thought that the piece had been fired, until told that it was struck by a rebel shell. And again if they had been solid shot which had struck it the piece would have been dismounted.

The letter also with other statements of several of the cannoneers, proves that it was the fourth piece of the battery, and that the gun was disabled by being struck by a rebel shell that exploded and killed two men that were in the act of loading it;

The rebels collected all their artillery and opened a concentrated fire upon us. It was terrible beyond description; the air was full of shell hissing and bursting. They came so thick and fast there was no dodging. Three shot or shell before they exploded struck my piece, one of them killing my No. 1 and No. 2, tearing the head off of No. 1, William Jones, and the shoulder and arm off of No. 2, Alfred G. Gardner. He lived a few minutes, and died shouting 'Glory to God!' and saying he was happy. He requested me to send his Bible to his wife, and tell her he died happy. He was a pious man, and he and I have been tenting together on this march.

Your brother,

[Signed,]   ALBERT STRAIGHT.

that the sergeant and other cannoneers, after it was
struck, tried to load it but failed, and the charge
was placed in the bore by the sergeant and stuck
there. (There is no proof to show whether it was the
same charge which Gardner had taken to put in or another one; but there was no ammunition found on the
ground after the piece was withdrawn from the field.)
And so the shot of that charge which was placed in
the gun by the sergeant remains firmly fixed in the
muzzle, and not a rebel shot, as some have claimed
it to be, and shot in there by one of the enemy's
guns during the cannonading of July 3, 1863, at the
battle of Gettysburg.

Sergeant Straight finding that the piece could not
be loaded reported it disabled, and was ordered by
Lieutenant Perrin to have it withdrawn from the
field to the rear, where the battery wagon and forge
were stationed.

About half past two o'clock P. M., Battery B's
fire began to slacken for want of men, and ammunition being about exhausted, and at quarter of three
P. M. a battery (Cowen's First New York Artillery)
came up to the ridge on the trot, wheeled into bat-

tery on the left of Battery B's position, and opened fire with spherical case shell on the enemy's line of infantry moving from the woods towards the Emmittsburg road in their front. Battery B at this time was relieved and ordered to the rear to where the battery wagon and forge were parked.

As the battery was limbering up and and retiring, the enemy's line of battle could be seen advancing from the woods on Seminary Ridge, three-fourths of a mile away. A line of skirmishers sprang forward lively, and with intervals well kept moved rapidly into the open fields, closely followed by a line of battle, then by another, and then by a third line.

General Gibbon's division, which was to stand the brunt of this assault, looked with eager gaze upon their foe marching forward with easy swinging step; and along the Union line the men were heard to exclaim : "Here they come ! Here they come !" Soon little puffs of smoke issued from the skirmish line as it came dashing forward firing in reply to our own skirmishers, never hesitating for an instant but driving our men before it or knocking them over by a biting fire. As they rose up to run in, the rebel skirmishers reached the fence along the Emmittsburg road. This was Pickett's advance, which carried a front of five hundred yards or more on that memorable charge of the Confederates against the Union centre. The repulse was one of the turning points against the confederates, and helped to break the backbone of the Rebellion.

As Battery B was leaving the line of battle, the field in rear of its position was being swept by the enemy's shot and bursting shell. The gun detachments and drivers to avoid this field took three pieces to the right, as they were facing to the rear, diagonally across towards the Taneytown Road. The other piece, of which the writer was lead driver at that time, instead of following the others went to the left down a cart path towards the same road.

We had not proceeded far when a shell exploded at our right, and a piece of it struck the wheel driver Charles G. Sprague on the forehead, cutting a gash from which the blood flowed down his face partly blinding him, so that he could not manage his horses. I asked the swing driver, Clarke L. Woodmansee, to take the wheel horses and let the swing horses go alone. He did so, relieving Sprague. Then we started on our way down the path again. The flash of bursting shell, and the screeching of shot, which were flying thick and fast around us, caused the swing horses now that they had no one to manage them to plunge first to one side then to the other, then backwards which greatly interfered with further progress. Looking to my left I saw one of our cannoneers, a detached man from the One Hundred and Fortieth Pennsylvania, Joseph Brackell, lying beside a large boulder rock. I called to him to come and drive them. He came and cleared the horses of the traces and mounted. This calmed the horses somewhat and we started on for the road again. When within a few rods of the road where the path descended, a shell at our right exploded, and a piece cut through the bowels of the off wheel horse, another striking the nigh swing horse, which Brackell was riding, on the gambrel joint, breaking the off leg. Still another piece swept across my off saddle cutting the nose-bags therefrom, whereby I lost my cooking utensils and extra rations I had in them. Whipping up my horses I shouted to the other

drivers, saying, " Let's get into the road ! " for they
wanted to stop. We continued on, the wheel horse
trampling on his bowels all the time, at every step,
as we swung around down into the road, which was
three feet lower than the field. Here the wheel
horse dropped dead, and we could go no further.
We had cleared the horses from the piece, and were
about changing the harnesses from dead and wounded
horses, so as to put the swing horse that was not
wounded in the place of the dead wheel horse, when
a shot came and struck the gun wheel taking out a
spoke and went screeching into the woods. This
was followed by a shell which exploded in the woods
in rear of us. This startled the horses and Woodmansee's horse went down the road, he after him.
Brackell, who had changed saddles, from his crippled horse to the sound one, now mounted and followed Woodmansee. The crippled horse seeing his
mate going hobbled on after, trying hard to keep up.
Being thus left alone I could do nothing there without help, so I mounted and went down the road to
find the battery, leaving the piece at the side of the
road. I found the road was anything but pleasant

3

to travel, for shot and shell were flying about quite lively.

On reaching a barn on the west side of the road used as headquarters of artillery brigade of the Second Corps, also a hospital, behind which were several staff officers, aids, and some cavalry, I asked for Battery B. They pointed down the road. Here I met Woodmansee, and together we kept on. We had not gone far before we heard a crash and report. On looking back saw the men and horses which had been back of the barn going in all directions. A shell had struck a corner of that barn and exploded, causing the stampede. A short distance from the barn in an opening among the woods on the east side of the Taneytown road and about a mile from our position in line of battle we found Battery B parked, and the men in bivouac, as some had shelter tents up. I reported that one of the pieces was left up in the road near General Meade's headquarters.

Late in the afternoon after the firing had subsided and all was quiet along the lines, Lieutenant Perrin with a detail of men, the writer being one of them, went back to the field of battle. Our troops had advanced from the position they had occupied when the battery left. The ground was strewn with torn haversacks, battered canteens, broken wheels of gun carriages, and piles of knapsacks and blankets, which silently told of the destruction which had visited the place.

The men gathered what accoutrements belonged to the battery, which had been left on the field when the battery withdrew. Returning to camp by way of the cart-path to the road where the third piece had been left it was not there. The dead horse lay beside the road, but the piece and harness were gone and we could get no information from men about there as to who carried it off, or in what direction it went. As it could not have fallen into the hands of the enemy being within our own lines, it was evident that some battery, ordnance or supply wagon drew it to the rear where other condemned ordnance was parked. As the number of the piece was not known to the officers of the battery, it was not returned to the battery, or any information obtained concerning it so far as the writer can learn.

Battery B's causalities in the two days' engage-

ments on the field were :   One officer Second Lieut.
Joseph S. Milne on detached service with Battery
A, Cushing's Fourth United States Artillery, mor-
tally wounded; died on or about the 8th or 10th
of July.   He was the only Rhode Island officer killed
at the battle of Gettysburg.   First Lieut. T. Fred.
Brown, commanding, was wounded July 2d, behind
the ear.   First Lieut. William S. Perrin, commanding
July 3d, was wounded in leg, but remained with the
battery in command.   Of the men there were five
killed, one taken prisoner, and one missing ; thirty-
two were wounded, nineteen of whom were sent to
the general hospital, where two died.   The others
were cared for in camp, their wounds being slight,
and in a few days they were on duty again.   Thus
the total loss was thirty-nine men.   The names of
those killed were :   July 2d, David B. King ; Ira
L. Bennett, of the Nineteenth Maine Regiment,
Michael Flynn, of the Fifteenth Massachusetts.
July 3d, Alfred G. Gardner and William Jones.

Wounded and sent to the hospital :   July 2d,
Orderly Sergt. John T. Blake, Sergt. Edwin A.
Chase, Corp. Henry H. Ballou, acting sergeant

(died), Corp. Chas. D. Worthington, Russell Austin, Mowry L. Andrews, Michael Duffy, George Mc-Gunnigle, William Maxcy, Charles H. Paine, Charles G. Sprague, Albert J. Whipple, Thomas W. Phillips, Bugler Eben S. Crowninshield. Detached men: Dyer Cady, Fifteenth Massachusetts; Lewis Moulton, Nineteenth Maine. On the 3d of July: Daniel N. Felt, John Green (died), George R. Matteson, wounded. Joseph Cassen was taken prisoner, and William H. Gallup was missing. There were sixty-five horses killed and wounded, and all the pieces were rendered unserviceable, condemned, and turned in to the ordnance department.

The fourth piece of the battery (the so-called Gettysburg gun), upon examination showed that the gun and gun carriage had been struck three times with shell, and also showed thirty-nine bullet marks, which serve to remind those who may look upon it of the ordeal through which it passed in that fearful strife. This gun with other condemned ordnance was sent to the Arsenal at Washington, D. C., there placed on exhibition, where it remained until May, 1874.

As the guns of Battery A, First Regiment Rhode Island Light Artillery, were upon examination found to be all right and serviceable after the battle, and as they had lost heavily in both men and horses, the remaining men and horses of Battery B were temporarily consolidated with them, forming the left section, with our First Lieut. William S. Perrin in command of section. And thus Battery B followed General Lee back into Virginia to the Rapidan River.

On August 8th, by orders Battery B left Battery A, proceeding to Bealton Station, and there on the 16th received a battery of four new light Napoleon brass pieces and caissons, a battery wagon and forge complete ; also harnesses and equipments for their horses from the ordnance department, making us a four-gun battery, with three commissioned officers. For men we had a number of volunteers from the infantry to serve as cannoneers, so we were again fully equipped for service, as Battery B, First Rhode Island Light Artillery, and remained in active service until the end of the war, being mustered out, June 12, 1865. In 1870 the surviving members of the battery held a reunion at Rocky Point, R. I., on the thirteenth day of August, that being the anniversary of the date of their muster into the United States service, and there formed a veteran association to hold annual reunions upon that day.   At the reunions held afterward the subject of this gun has been an animated matter of discussion.   Through efforts of the members of the Association, the citizens of Rhode Island, and Hon. Henry B. Anthony, late senator from this State, Congress honored the Association with the privilege of placing this memento of the battle of Gettysburg in the care and protection of the State of Rhode Island.

In 1874, Daniel C. Taylor, then president of Battery B, Veteran Association, was largely instrumental in having the gun turned over from the general government to the State, and, with Lieut. James E. Chase and J. Borden Lewis, was appointed a committee to go to Washington, D. C., to receive the gun ; also a copy of the act of Congress giving the gun to the State.   This copy was obtained by Senator Henry B. Anthony, who had it suitably engrossed and presented to the Association.

The following is a copy of the act of Congress :

AN ACT AUTHORIZING THE SECRETARY OF WAR TO DELIVER TO THE STATE AUTHORITIES OF RHODE ISLAND A CERTAIN GUN.

Be it enacted by the Senate and House of Representatives of the United States of America in Congress assembled:

That the Secretary of War be and he is hereby authorized to deliver, if the same can be done without detriment to the government, to the proper authorities of the State of Rhode Island, a certain gun marked Battery B First Regiment of Rhode Island Light Artillery, battle of Gettysburg, for the purpose of being placed among the achives of that State.

JAMES G. BLAINE,
Speaker of House of Representatives.

MATT. H. CARPENTER,
President of the Senate Pro. Tem.

Approved February 19, 1874.

U. S. GRANT.

At Providence, R. I., on May 21, 1874, there was a grand military demonstration on the reception of Battery B's relic, and the delivery of the gun to the State, which took place under very trying and moist aspects of the weather, with the following committees in charge viz. :

Governor Henry Howard, Gen. Chas. R. Dennis, Hon. J. M. Addeman in behalf of the State; Mayor Thomas A. Doyle, Col.

N. Van Slyck, Henry R. Barker, in behalf of the city; Col. A. C. Eddy, George R. Drowne, Lieut. James E. Chace, John F. Hanson, Finance Committee; Col. J. Albert Monroe, Col. E. H. Rhodes, J. Borden Lewis, Programme Committee; Gen. Charles R. Dennis, Edwin Metcalf, Silas G. Tucker, Reception Committee; Lieut. James E. Chase; Daniel C. Taylor, President; J. Borden Lewis, Gun Committee; Col. J. Albert Monroe, Chief Marshal; Col. E. H. Rhodes, Chief of Staff.

The patter of the rain Thursday morning was anything but merry music to the Battery B boys who heard it, and to the veterans and militia who were to join them in the parade and demonstration.

Everything looked blue to the boys except the sky, and that was dull enough, while the rain poured as if it had set in for a long storm and was taking it easy. Old Probabilities was anxiously consulted but he had no encouragement to offer. But in spite of the weather flags were thrown to the breeze from public and private flag-staffs as if to encourage us.

In front of the Soldiers and Sailors Monument on Exchange Place a stand had been erected for the formal exercises, with a national flag flying at each corner, and in the centre a banner bearing the clover leaf (Trefoil) of the Second Corps, under which in a scroll was the thrilling word, "GETTYSBURG." There was little evidence that this stand would be wanted or used that day.

The marshal and commanding officers of various organizations met together to consult about postponement. Postponement meant almost certain failure, while if carried out the demonstration if not what was expected and wished, would at least have the merit of spirit and punctuality, and show that when the veterans take hold of anything they mean business.

Before a decision was reached the cars arrived from Westerly bringing the Westerly Rifle Battalion of one hundred and three men, under command of Col. A. N. Crandall, who, undaunted by the weather, had come to parade. This was encouraging certainly, and before the enthusiasm created by this had subsided, the boat arrived from Newport with two bands and the Newport Artillery and Veteran Association. More encouragement and matters began to assume more life.

Lieutenant-Colonel Bullock of the First Light Infantry Regiment on being asked what his command

would do, quickly replied, " We shall parade if you
do." And the same reply was received from the
United Train of Artillery, the Marine Artillery, and
many of the other organizations. With all this encouragement and the fact that most of the men had
come prepared to parade, the matter was decided
and the order given : " Prepare for Parade."

The rain, however, caused some changes in the
proceedings, the route of march was cut short, and
Music Hall was engaged for the exercises intended
for Exchange Place.

An arrangement was made for an artillery signal
at two o'clock to inform the different organizations
what to do. At half past one o'clock it let up somewhat, and just about two o'clock the Marine Artillery
marched into Exchange Place and fired the signal
gun, which said to those in waiting,—Parade.

At this time a large force of the umbrella brigade
lined the sidewalks, while every window on Exchange Place was crowded to the utmost, and matters
soon began to assume a lively aspect.

The militia was promptly on hand, soon followed
by the other organizations arriving from different

directions, and all were assigned positions by the chief marshal and aides.

THE LINE.

Col. J. Albert Monroe, Chief Marshal.
Col. Elisha H. Rhodes, Chief of Staff.

———

First Division, Mounted Troops.

Lieutenant-Colonel Stephen Brownell, Assistant Marshal.
Providence Horse Guards, Col. J. Lippitt Snow
commanding, and staff of six field officers.
Co. A, Capt. Geo. B. Inman, three officers and fifteen men.
Co. B, Captain David Lester, two officers and fifteen men.
Pawtucket Horse Guards, Major J. W. Leckie
commanding, staff and line officers, thirty-five men.
Tower Light Battery, Pawtucket, Major Daniel Briggs
commanding, one officer and sixteen men.

———

Second Division, Mounted Light Battery.

Adjutant J. M. Hull, Assistant Marshal.
Providence Marine Corps of Artillery, Lieutenant-Colonel
Robert Grosvenor commanding, eight officers and
six pieces and caissons fully manned.

———

Third Division, Veteran Associations.

Lieut. James E. Chace, Assistant Marshal.
Platoon of Police, Sergeant Warner.
American Band, D. W. Reeves, leader, twenty-eight pieces.

First Regiment Rhode Island Veteran Association, thirty men.

Second Regiment Rhode Island Veteran Association,
Col. Horatio Rogers, President, fifty men.

Third Regiment Rhode Island Veteran Association,
Gen. Charles R. Brayton, President, sixty men.

Ninth Regiment Rhode Island Veteran Association,
J. T. Pitman, President, twenty men.

Eleventh Regiment Rhode Island Veteran Association,
Robert Fessenden, President, twenty men.

First Regiment Rhode Island Light Artillery Veteran Association, I. R. Sheldon, Vice-President, forty men.

Ives Post, No. 13, G. A. R., R. F. Nicola, commander,
twenty-five men.

Battery B, First Rhode Island Light Artillery Veteran Association, forty men.

———

As escorts to the Gettysburg Gun.

Lieutenant Gideon Spencer, commanding.

Sergt. John F. Hanson, orderly.

The Gun Detachment with Gun.

Edwin A. Chace, sergeant of piece.

Corporal Edward B. Whipple, gunner.

No. 1. Benj. A. Burlingame. No. 2. Josiah McMeekin.

No. 3. Joseph Cassin. No. 4. Chas. D. Worthington.

No. 5. John Delavan. No. 6. Charles Cornell.

No. 7. Charles J. Rider.

Drivers, Joseph Cole, lead; Levi J. Cornell, swing; Stephen
Collins, wheel.

4

John Healy, with the old headquarters flag of the Artillery Brigade of the Second Corps.

The Fourth Division, Invited Guests.

Sergt. Silas G. Tucker, Assistant Marshal.

Governor Henry Howard, Lieut.-Governor C. C. Van Zandt, Adjutant-General H. LeFavour, in carriage.

Colonel Waterman, Colonel Barstow, Colonel Nightingale.

Colonel Robinson of Governor's staff, mounted.

Maj.-Gen. Wm. R. Walker, Colonels Jenks and Fisk, Majors Tillinghast, Deming and Pierce, of his staff, in carriage.

Q. M. Gen. Chas. R. Dennis, Surgeon-General King, in carriage.

Brigadier-General Burdick, Chaplain Jones, Surgeon Turner, Captains Marvell and Sisson of his staff, mounted.

Brig.-Gen. Frederick Miller, and Capt. A. E. Greene,

Capt. W. B. Vincent of his staff, in carriage, all in new uniforms.

Major-General Warren, U. S. A., commander of Fifth Army Corps. Major-General Averill, U. S. A., commander Cavalry Division. Col. A. P. Blunt, Quartermaster, U. S. A.

Brig.-Gen. John G. Hazard, U. S. Volunteers.

Col. W. H. Reynolds of First Regiment Rhode Island Light Artillery.

Brev. Lieut.-Col. J. H. Rice, U. S. A., Maj. C. E. Rice, U. S. A.

Capt. C. E. Bowers, Massachusetts Volunteers.

Capt. N. N. Noyes, Boston Light Infantry.

Capt. T. L. Harlow, Company C Fourth Battalion of Infantry, and H. E. Hotchkiss, of New Haven, Connecticut.

James Foley, of New York, and C. E. Tucker, Blackstone, Massachusetts, all in carriages.

Fifth Division State Militia.

Capt. C. Henry Barney, Assistant Marshal.

Drum corps of eight pieces.

Westerly Rifle Battalion, Col. A. N. Crandall commanding,
with eight field and staff officers.

Co. A, Capt. A. B. Dyer, four officers and forty-eight men.

Co. B, Capt. J. A. Brown, four officers and thirty-five men.

Burnside National Guards, Maj. Geo. H. Black commanding,
three field and staff officers.

Co. A, Capt. W. H. Scott, three officers and twenty-six men.

Co. B, Capt. Thomas Brinn, three officers and thirty men.

Co. C, Capt. Lewis Kenegee, three officers and thirty-two men.

Newport Brass Band, J. E. O. Smith, leader, twenty-six pieces.

United Train of Artillery, Col. Oscar Lapham, commanding,
six field and staff officers.

Co. A, Capt. G. A. Dodge, three officers and twenty men.

Co. B, Capt. F. S. McCausland, two officers and twenty-two men.

Co. C, Capt. C. G. Cahoone, two officers and twenty men.

Gilmore's, Pawtucket Band, T. J. Allen, leader,
twenty-two pieces.

Rhode Island Guards, Colonel J. Costine, commanding,
three staff and field officers.

Co. A, J. H. McGann, three officers and thirty-eight men.

Co. D, Capt. J. E. Curren, three officers and thirty men.

Co. G, Lieut. William McPherson, two officers and
thirty-six men.

Co. H, Capt. James Leary, three officers and thirty-two men.

First Light Infantry Drum Corps, G. W. Lewis, leader,
twelve men.

First Light Infantry Regiment, Col. R. H. I. Goddard
commanding, four field and staff officers.
Co. A, Capt. J. H. Kendrick,
three officers and twenty-eight men.
Co. B, Capt. E. F. Annable, three officers and twenty-seven men.
Co. C, Captain Wm. Frankland, three officers and
thirty-five men.
Co. D, Capt. A. H. Hartwell, two officers and twenty-five men.
Drum Major Charles Whitters, of Hartford.
National Band, Wm. E. White, leader, twenty-seven pieces.
Slocum Light Guards, Lieut.-Col. Benj. P. Swarts
commanding, two staff officers.
Co. A, Capt. W. B. W. Hallett, three officers and twenty men.
Co. B, Lieutenant B. McSoley, two officers and twenty men.

The First Light Infantry Regiment wore their fatigue uniforms, with red blankets belted at the waist. They had as
their guests, Col. B. B. Martin, Maj. J. B. Childs, Adjt. B. M.
Bosworth, Jr., and Quartermaster F. E. Dana, of the Warren
Artillery, Col. Julies Sayles, Lieut. Col. J. D. Seabury, Maj. Howard Smith, Capt. Silas De Blois, Q. M. Benj. Marsh, Surgeon
Henry E. Turner, Paymaster George H. Wilson of the Newport
Artillery Veteran Association and Lieutenant-Colonel Sherman
of the Newport Artillery. The United Train of Artillery were
attired in fatigue uniforms, with dress caps and pompon, and
had for their guests the Westerly Rifle Regiment, the Newport
Brass Band and the field and staff officers of the Pawtucket
Light Guards. The Slocum Light Guards were in fatigue dress
and overcoats, and their guests were Captain Morse, of Company G, Third Regiment Massachusetts Volunteer Militia, the

Taunton Guards, of Taunton, Mass., Capt. N. N. Noyes, of Boston Light Infantry, and Captain Hanlon and Lieutenant Fallon of the Boston Tigers, Fourth Massachusetts Volunteer Militia.

A pleasant feature to the Battery boys, was the presence in the Association line of the old headquarters flag of the Artillery Brigade of the Second Corps.

At 3.15 P. M. the column moved in good order through the following streets: Dorrance, up Westminster, Mathewson, Washington, Franklin, down High to Broad, Weybosset to Market Square, countermarching over the bridge through Washington Row to Exchange Place, Dorrance to Westminster, up to Music Hall, which was reached at four o'clock, and though the rain was then falling briskly the streets were lined with interested spectators. The line was a fine one all things considered, and gave evidence of what the demonstration would have been had the weather been more favorable.

At Music Hall the American Band, D. W. Reeves, leader, was stationed in the seats between the organ and the platform. On the platform were His Excellency Gov. Henry Howard and staff, Lieut. Gov. C.

C. Van Zandt, Maj.-Gen. A. E. Burnside, Maj.-Gen.
W. R. Walker and staff; Brig.-Gen. F. Miller and
staff; Rev. Carlton A. Staples, Orator of the Day;
Rev. D. H. Greer, Chaplain of the Day; Daniel C.
Taylor, President of Battery B Veteran Association,
Brig.-Gen. John G. Hazard, as presiding officer, and
the different committees of arrangements.

After music by the American Band and prayer
by Chaplain Greer, the Chairman, General Hazard,
introduced Daniel C. Taylor, President of Battery B
Veteran Association for the delivery of the gun to
the State, which he said should make every Rhode
Islander proud.

President Taylor, who was warmly received upon
coming forward, then formally delivered the gun to
to the State authorities in the following address :

YOUR EXCELLENCY: As presiding officer of Battery B Veteran Association, the duty devolves upon me to place in your
custody and keeping, as chief executive officer of this State this
piece of ordnance, consecrated to liberty, and baptized in the
blood of Rhode Island's sons. And to impress more fully upon
your heart, if possible, the sacredness of this honored relic to
us, I desire to give you a brief history of this gun from the time
of its reception by us as a part of our battery until the present.

During the Peninsular campaign the battery consisted of four Parrott guns and two brass howitzers. After the terrible seven days battle which terminated at Malvern Hill, and the Army of the Potomac found rest at Harrison Landing, on the James River, Va., the vents of our guns were found to be in such a condition as to render the guns unfit for service. They were therefore condemned, and their places supplied upon the 31st of July, 1862, by a park of new guns, consisting of six brass twelve-pound Napoleons, of which this gun was one.

Upon the reorganization of the Army of the Potomac Battery B was attached to the Second Brigade, General Gorman, Second Division, General Sedgwick, Second Corps, General Sumner, which position they held during the war, notwithstanding the various changes which took place of commanders of brigade, division or corps. The battery with this piece and others, was at the shelling of the town of Fredericksburg, Va., Dec. 11, 1862. Stationed at the right of the Lacy House, on a bluff overlooking the town, it fired three hundred and eighty-four rounds of shot and shell upon the town and the rebel rifle-pits, when the pontoon bridge was being laid. On the morning of December 12th, at six o'clock, we crossed the bridge and entered the town, being the first battery to cross at this place.

At the battle of Fredericksburg, December 13th, the battery was at four o'clock in the afternoon ordered to the front, and took position on the left of the road at the brick house in front of the stone wall, and here did good service. The battery did similar service at the second battle of Fredericksburg or Mayre's Heights.

About the 18th of June commenced the skirmishes which terminated in the great struggle of Gettysburg.

July 1st the battery with the Second Corps arrived within three miles of the town, and July 2d was assigned position in battery about ten o'clock in line of the Second Corps and to the left of Cemetery Hill, our line being joined by the Third Corps on our left. In the afternoon while the Third Corps was engaged, the battery was advanced to the right and front, and engaged a rebel battery at once, and in this position the battery was charged upon, and forced to retire to the rear of the lines of infantry.

On the 3d of July the battery and this gun took part in that great artillery duel just before Pickett's grand charge, and it was in this fierce storm of shot and shell that this piece was struck by a shell which exploded and killed two men in the act of loading it. This shell disabled the gun so that it could not be loaded. It was condemned and sent to Washington, D. C. At the Arsenal it was placed on exhibition, where it remained until this time; and, sir, I am proud to say that to me has been accorded the privilege of obtaining through our honored senator, Henry B. Anthony and others, this valued memento for the people of Rhode Island, and as an ever pleasant reminder to our children of that loyalty and fidelity to duty that actuated their sires, and may they learn and profit by the experience of their fathers. And in behalf of my comrades I desire to express the wish that this piece of ordnance may be deposited upon the green in front of the State House in this city within an appropriate enclosure, and that it be protected during the inclement season by a suitable covering. And with the strong conviction that our wishes will be carried out, I leave the piece in your possession and care.

The address was very attentively listened to, and at its close was very earnestly applauded.

Governor Howard who remained standing during President Taylor's address responded as follows :

MR. PRESIDENT: Rhode Island accepts the honorable trust which you confide to her. She takes into her faithful keeping this mute witness, this interesting memento of the most decisive and glorious struggle known to the annals of freedom. More than this, reminded by its presence of the eventful scene which attended that triumph of our arms, of the heroic devotion and valor of her own ever honored sons, recalling the noble and resolute ardor of patriotism which impelled them to stand an impregnable barrier between a flushed and superior force and the menaced firesides of the North, she assumes with the trust the higher guardianship of the holy memories and associations which this occasion revives, recognizing in the inspiration of the hour a lesson and a mandate for the future, she dedicates herself to the pious care of guarding with the reverent tenderness of a mother's love, the fair fame of those who stood for her and the nation on the ensanguined crest of Gettysburg. Survivors of the field, your State folds you in its grateful arms to-day. Spirits above who poured out your young lives in availing though costly sacrifice for us, receive the inadequate homage of our saddened remembrance and our eternal gratitude.

The governor's remarks elicited another spirited manifestation of approval.

The chairman, General Hazard, then introduced the Orator of the Day, Rev. Carlton A. Staples, late Chaplain United States Volunteers, who delivered the following eloquent oration :

REV. C. A. STAPLES'S ORATION.

The occasion which has brought us together is one of no ordinary interest. This gun which has now been delivered up to the State of Rhode Island is a sacred relic of the war which saved the Union. . By the valor of your sons it did good service in that war, and in the blood of your sons it was baptized. Let us call it then a precious, a sacred memento. For suffering borne in a noble cause, sacrifice cheerfully made for the highest interest of man, life yielded up heroically in defence of honor, of country, of freedom, make any object or spot sacred to the human breast. Hence the undying interest which gathers about every place where martyrs have suffered or heroes have died for the truth. Hence the reverence with which we trace the footsteps of the first settlers on this wild New England shore. Hence the solemn feeling that steals over the soul at Thermopylae and Marathon, at Bannockburn and Marston Moor, at Bunker Hill and Valley Forge. The heroism, suffering, and blood of men in behalf of country and right sanctify the meanest object and glorify the humblest place.

What but a life like Christ's, laid upon the altar of a love for man so broad, sweet and high, could have changed an instru-

ment of torture and shame like the cross into an object of inspiration and of beauty? Since the war we have felt a new
respect for the musket, the cannon, and the soldier. Not that
war seems less dreadful, or, when waged in behalf of injustice
and for territorial conquest, less wicked. No pen has ever ade-
quately pictured its horrors. No christian heart but shrinks from
it as from the fires of hell. No real soldier who has been in one
battle ever desires to be in another. But horrible as war always
is and must be; there are things worse than war—national dis-
grace and dishonor are worse; national indifference to principles of justice, to the inalienable rights of man, and all the in-
terests of his higher nature, are worse. Better war with all its
suffering agony and loss, than a peace of moral stagnation and
decay. We are fond of saying that "The pen is mightier than
the sword." But when the pen is enlisted in the cause of rob-
bery and oppression, it produces a state of society at last which
only the sword can purify. Thought may be a weapon stronger
than cannon balls. But wrong thinking, and wrong acting, to
which it so often leads, sometimes necessitates the use of cannon balls to beat down the falsehood and let in the light of
truth. It is right thinking, and, what is nobler, right living,
that are to sheath every sword at last, and stop the mouth of
every gun. Unless the pen, therefore, be guided by an intelli-
gent mind, and an honest and good heart, these instruments of
destruction will be needed to undo its baleful work.

Looking at the War of the Rebellion from this point of view,
and in this connection, as we stand around this sacred memento,
we feel towards it something of the tenderness and respect of
the Arab for the noble steed that has saved him from his mortal
foe.

For this gun, manned by our brothers and sons on many a
battlefield, has beaten back the hosts that sought our country's
ruin. At Gettysburg it saved our Northern cities from being
sacked and burned, and our homes from devastation and
death.

With its hundred fellows it kept our line firm and strong on
that momentous day, and broke to pieces the ranks of the advancing foe. Those guns and bayonets in the hands of our
valiant men knocked the shackles from the limbs of three
million slaves, and made the Declaration of Independence something more than a glittering generality in this land. They
swept away as in a whirlwind of flame a thousand old false-
hoods and wrongs, and let in the light which pulpit, platform
and press had resolutely barred out. They made it possible
for an American citizen to call his country a land of equal rights
and privileges without a flush of shame.

Take this gun, then, and place it among the proudest archives
of the State. Cherish it as a precious legacy from the men
who bore it into the fore-front of the battle, and laid down their
lives in serving it there. Tell your children and your children's children the story of its triumph; a triumph not of men
over men, but of truth over error; right over wrong; freedom over slavery. And bid them remember that whenever they
cling to false principles and base practice in the conduct of the
government, embody the idea in law that any class, condition or sect may have superior privileges or power, and array
themselves against the reform of any injustice or corruption in
the State, they are building up a condition of society, which, at
last will surely let loose the dogs of war. For so deep in the soul

has the Almighty planted the love of justice, and of equality before the law, that no community can outrage that sentiment even in its treatment of the lowest members without kindling in its own bosom the fire of ceaseless strife, and destroying the fabric of its own peace and power, "First pure, then peaceable," says the Apostle. It is as truly the divine order in social and political life as it is in the experience of the individual soul.

Of the history of the battery to which this gun belonged, it does not need that I should speak. The story of its organization, its long marches, its fierce and bloody conflicts with the foe, its faithful service and its heroic sacrifice, has been already told by one who bore a part in these things, and by whom they are much better understood.

Among those who lost their lives in this engagement we would mention Second Lieut. Joseph S. Milne, a gentleman and a soldier, who is said to have endeared himself to the hearts of his brother officers, and commanded the love and respect of every member of the battery. He was born at Fall River, Mass., his father being a minister of the Gospel, and at the time of his death his mother was engaged in teaching a contraband school at Hilton Head. A short time before he was employed at the *Post* and *Herald* office in this city, and was the only officer the battery lost during the service.

The men shot at this gun were William Jones, a native of Boston, Mass., one of the original members of the battery, and Alfred G. Gardner, a recruit.

All this has passed into history, and occupies an honorable place in the record made by the State of Rhode Island during the war.

5

But there is an unwritten history lying behind these external events which gives them their real significance and glory. Though this gun be forever silenced, though its voice will never again be heard in thunders of war, yet it speaks to us and those who are to come after us in tones that cannot be misunderstood. It tells us of what manner of men they were who came forth at the call of their country, and bared their bosoms to shield her from death. Its dumb lips are eloquent to minds that can grasp and hearts that can feel the real nobility of their spirits. Truer, braver souls never went up to God in the fiery chariot of battle than they. I know that they came from humble homes, that their hands were hardened by the toil of the workshop, the factory and the farm. I know that thousands of them had no expectation of rising above the humblest place in the ranks, and were content to stand there and to bear on their shoulders the awful burdens of war that their country might be saved. But in the main they were men of royal stuff. They went out from good homes. They had been trained in the common schools and taught to reverence the principles of justice and of truth. They knew what was at stake in the war. They were thoughtful men. They were reared in the love of peace. All their aspirations and plans in life belonged to peaceful arts and industries.

But when the call came how grandly they responded to it, and through the long, dreadful years of the war, in camps, in hospitals, in rebel prisons, under delay and defeat, how patient, how true and how firm they were. In victory how magnanimous, in suffering how heroic, in death how peaceful! As I call to mind the scene on the Plains of Abraham when Wolfe

died in the moment of victory, saying, "I am content," and
Nelson, on the deck of his ship, expiring just as the awful battle had been won, serene and happy, I see the glory of that
spirit in man which rises above the horrors of war, and is
mightier than death. But I have seen a spirit as high, serene
and happy in the humblest man of our armies, dying in dreary
hospitals and camps, well knowing that no monument would
ever be raised to their memory, nor mother, wife, nor friend
look upon their graves. "Tell my wife and children," said a
dying soldier shot down on picket duty at night, "that I have
done the best I could." "You are dying for your country,"
said one who knelt beside him. "That is what I came here
for," was the reply, and so he fell asleep.

And what can be more glorious than the spirit of Alfred
Gardner, who stood beside this gun under that terrific fire at
Gettysburg, and placed that shot in its muzzle which a rebel
shell caused to be sealed there forever? He fell at his post, his
arm and shoulder torn from his side; but with the other arm
he drew from his pocket a Testament and a little book which
he carried with him to press flowers, and handing them to his
sergeant said, "Give these to my wife, and tell her that I died
happy—glory, glory, hallelujah!" Nelson when dying remembered his mistress, and commended her to the care of his country. Gardner remembered his Testament, his herbarium and
his wife, and departed shouting, "Glory, hallelujah," amid the
roaring of two hundred guns.

Do not such men deserve to be remembered with prayers
and tears of gratitude? Thousands as heroic, as faithful, as
grand, fell in that awful strife. Call them "hirelings," "the

refuse of our cities?" Shame on such words and all who utter them! Call them the kings and priests of liberty. Call them the saviors of republican institutions and the servants of the living God. On such an occasion as this it is well for us to re- member what it has cost to save republican institutions in this land, and free our country from the curse of slavery. I speak not of the millions of treasure swallowed up and lost in the war; of the mountains of debt heaped upon us and the burdens of taxation laid upon our industry and our wealth; nor of the suffering and agony which it carried to ten thousand homes, filling them with loneliness and gloom, but of the cost in valu- able lives, in men who added something to the intelligence, the patriotism, the conscience, the moral integrity of the country. We have lost not only countless millions of money and prop- erty, but an aggregate of moral character and influence a thou- sand times more valuable. The best blood of the country was poured out on the battlefields of the war. No man can tell how much poorer we are as a people, in conscience, in honor, in manliness for its loss. There is less political integrity among us ; less care that high public offices be filled by compe- tent and worthy men; less fidelity to principle in the use of the ballot ; less vigilance in protecting the sacredness of the ballot. There is greater greed for riches, and less scruple about the means used to gain them. There is a lower sense of honor in the discharge of sacred trusts, and a deeper craving for sensa- tional excitement and extravagant display; a lower tone in social and political life, due largely to the loss of moral charac- ter incurred by the death of so many thousands of our noblest men. We miss them sorely in our homes and in all the pleas-

ant walks of life. But more than this, we miss them in the
pulse of the public conscience, of mercantile honor, of legisla-
tive purity, of corporate and municipal faith. An approximate
estimate can be made of the money cost, but who can gauge
the moral cost of saving the Union?

And is it not well that we should be reminded in the presence
of such a relic as this of what remains to be done in the work
of our country's salvation?

The nation was saved in that awful crisis by a great valor and
terrible sacrifice.

And we are all too ready to cry out, "It is finished," and
shut our eyes in security and peace, forgetting that it needs a
continual saving. We think the cannon and the bayonet closed
up the work forever at Appomattox Court-House, leaving us
all free to pursue our private schemes of gain or pleasure. But
I tell you a greater peril than rebel armies will soon be upon us
if we yield ourselves up to this false sense of security. "A
government of the people, by the people, and for the people,"
requires the constant interest and vigilant activity of the people. Without them it must soon fall a prey to the machinations
of bad men. Without them the filth of the gutters will rise up
to the high places of power in its cities, its halls of legislation
and its courts. If eternal vigilance be the price of liberty it is
also the price of purity and safety in a republican government.
And if we care so little for this grand heritage, received from
the fathers and preserved at the cost of so much treasure and
blood, that we will not give a day in the year from our business
to prevent bribery at the polls and help elect good men to all
offices of trust and responsibility; if we care so little what

kind of men represent us in the City Council, in the Legislature and in Congress, what kind of sentiments they utter or laws they make, that we never look into their private life or hold them to account for the course they pursue in their public actions; if we are too indifferent or too busy to pay any regard to the country's welfare in such vital matters as these, who will say we deserve to have a country, or that we are worthy of the great legacy that has been bestowed upon us, or the tremendous sacrifices that have been made for us? I see cause for alarm in this growing neglect of political duties, and the consequent corruption in official. life. I see a more insidious, a more deadly foe to the country's welfare in this easy, indifferent spirit which sits content by the fireside, while bad men worm their way into power, than in rebel bayonets and cannon. It is the stronghold of base measures and corrupt men. It is a poor tribute we pay to the memory of our dead heroes, when we scatter a few flowers on their graves, if we are careless and thoughtless in the exercise of our political rights.

May I not appropriately on this occasion use the thought of our martyr president in that sublime speech at Gettysburg? It is not our poor words and prayers which make this gun a consecrated memento. It has been already consecrated by our brothers' suffering and blood. But let us here consecrate ourselves to political fidelity, purity and justice, that we may carry on the work which they begun, and transmit untarnished to our children what they died to save.

With one other thought I will close. It has already been explained to you how this gun was loaded, and why it can never be discharged. Brave men have struggled for it in the carnage and madness of battle. Once it was lost and then recaptured. Its voice is now forever silenced, and its place is to be amid the great enterprises and busy industries of this beautiful city.

It symbolizes, as we proudly hope, the future history of our country and the final destiny of the world. The strife in which it played so noble a part is over. Its lesson must never be forgotten, but its animosities must be buried in mutual helpfulness and kindness. They were our brothers; as honest, as brave, and as conscientious as we.

On those battlefields the Bible was met by the Bible, and prayer by prayer. They believed in their cause as firmly as we, and sacrificed even more unselfishly.

They lost and we won, because they were wrong and we were right, and they were poor and we were rich. The cause of the strife was a mutual sin. Scarcely less was our guilt than theirs, and scarcely less have we suffered than they.

One thing we must insist upon, cost what it may, that this is a land of equal rights and privileges for all its people. Holding that as forever sacred, let us bear and forbear, give and forgive, scatter flowers on our dead and on their dead, for they were equally heroic, equally true to what they believed was right, and they perished for a common crime. Every point that justice requires let it be yielded cheerfully and promptly, and let all our conduct towards them be inspired as I think in the main it has been, by magnanimity and christian kindness.

A glorious era will it be when all nations shall lay down their arms, and a code of international law shall bind them to everlasting peace. We catch glimpses of the dawning of that day in a growing public sentiment for a congress of nations before which all the differences of nations shall be tried. The example of England and the United States in the Geneva arbitration has deepened that sentiment throughout the world. It is sure to prevail at last. For all the forces of civilization and christianity are on its side. The telegraph, the steam engine, the printing press, are fast binding all races and nations together, creating a common interest by causing them all to suffer together or rejoice.

War of nation upon nation will become a universal calamity by this interlinking of interest and sympathy; and the doctrine of Christ become a visible reality in a brotherhood of nations. When that glorious day has come, as come it surely will, may this gun again find voice to speak, and in thunder tones utter the people's joy.

The interesting occasion was brought to a close with music—"Auld Lang Syne"—by the American Band.

There was no re-formation of the line as a whole. The several veteran associations and the militia proceeded separately to their respective quarters, and thus ended the great demonstration, which was nobly carried out despite the disagreeable weather. At the close of the parade the Gettysburg gun was placed on exhibition in the *Journal* Office on Weybosset street, by the battery boys where it attracted much attention

from crowds of persons who eagerly thronged to more
closely view the great war relic and curiosity. The
storm cleared away after the parade, but that was not
much comfort to the participants in the day's demonstration. But the rain, however, was not allowed to
dampen the ardor and enthusiasm of our Rhode Island
veterans, and during the entire movements of the
afternoon their general deportment was excellent.

www.ingramcontent.com/pod-product-compliance
Lightning Source LLC
Chambersburg PA
CBHW021233260626
47172CB00002B/737